THE HOODED QUILT SERIES

———— Book 1 ————

*Night Rhythms*

To Henry & Charlie,
Many wonderful
adventures to you!

BOOK ONE

## THE HOODED QUILT SERIES

1

# NIGHT RHYTHMS

WRITTEN BY

## SHALANDA R. SIMS

INKWATER
PRESS

PORTLAND • OREGON
INKWATERPRESS.COM

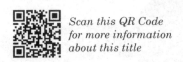
*Scan this QR Code*
*for more information*
*about this title*

Library of Congress Control Number: 2017903488

Publisher: Inkwater Press | www.inkwaterpress.com

Paperback ISBN-13 978-1-62901-463-0 | ISBN-10 1-62901-463-X
Kindle       ISBN-13 978-1-62901-464-7 | ISBN-10 1-62901-464-8


Printed in the U.S.A.

3 5 7 9 10 8 6 4 2

*For Sy*

# Contents

# BaD DREam

I n the dark room with only the streetlights shining in through blinds on the window, looking at the shadowed silhouette of my body reflecting off the wall, I knelt beside my parents' bed on my mother's side, lightly shaking her arm.

"Mama, I'm scared."

I know when you're ten years old you're not supposed to be afraid of certain things, but if you knew the dream I had, you'd be afraid too. Lucky for me, Mama always knew exactly what to do to make me feel better.

Sitting up from her good sleep as if an alarm playing soft music just went off, Mama opened her eyes.

 1

"What is it?" Still adjusting her eyes, she said, "Did you have a bad dream?"

That's the first thing she asked when I came to her in the middle of the night, as if she knew I'd had a bad dream. Now, with clear focus on me, I was certain she saw the white part of my eyes surrounding my big brown pupils nodding up and down. Pulling me in close with one arm and gently rubbing my back with the other, she asked, "Do you want to tell me about it?"

I held on tightly to her hand and she guided both of us toward my bedroom. We walked quietly and whispered so as not to wake my father, who only had a few more hours to sleep before going to work, and trying not to bother my younger brother, Thurston, whose room sat adjacent to mine.

My room was softened by a pretty pink, angelic nightlight and stuffed animals that lay organized in a corner, stacked upon shelves. Old Barbie dolls stood still in their boxes on purple shelves right above the animals. On the wall next to my bed glowed an intriguing tree painted in different shades of brown, with family names written in italic on metallic gold- and green-leaf paper with replicas of famous African-American art sporadically placed amongst the names.

It was an art project Mama did with my

brother and me. Thurston argued the tree should be in his room, but when Mama told him he'd be expected to learn and recite the history on the wall, he quickly changed his mind. I only wanted the tree because it was shiny. It made me feel happy. I didn't want to learn about every person and picture, but Mama insisted I didn't have a choice in the matter and that I'd thank her later. That was two years ago, when I was eight. I hadn't thanked her yet.

Sitting on my daybed, I plopped my head on Mama's arm and exhaled, "It was horrible. I was walking down our street, and all of a sudden, it wasn't our street anymore. It was a street I never saw before. There were kids I've never seen. They looked weird. They kept coming toward me. My heart was beating fast. I was so nervous I started running away. Then they chased after me, but I saw our house again, so I ran inside, but it wasn't our house. Then I woke up."

Offering a soft smile, stroking my wavy hair, Mama said, "Wow, that was some dream. Did you watch any scary shows this afternoon or read any strange stories?"

"Well, there was this one book we read in class today, *New Kid on the Block*," I explained. "It was about a boy who moved to

a new neighborhood. All the kids thought he was an alien because he looked different."

Mama steadily caressed my head. "It sounds like that story had a lot to do with your dream."

I didn't want to tell her the rest of my dream. It was even scarier than the beginning. "Mama, it seemed real." Still afraid as if I were five years old again, I asked, "Can you please lie with me? I can't go back to sleep. My brain keeps thinking about my dream and my heart is beating out of my pajamas."

She tilted her head to the side and gave me a different, more intense look. "Sure, honey, I will stay in your room until you fall asleep."

Mama pulled the blanket back for me to slip under, then she grabbed a throw blanket for herself from the linen closet in the hall next to my room and cuddled close.

I dozed off until I felt Mama gently moving out of bed. Sliding on her pink slippers, she headed for the door. "Mama, don't go."

She turned around with her pointer finger against her lips then motioned for me to come to her. Quietly, I got out of bed and went with Mama. The two of us entered the kitchen and I rested at the table. She always tried to figure out ways to make me comfortable.

She put the kettle on the stove for hot cocoa.

4

Whenever I wasn't feeling good, hot cocoa usually put me right to sleep. But I refused.

"I don't want any hot cocoa."

I know it was just a dream, but it seemed real, and I wasn't willing to go back to bed, no matter how tired I was. I didn't want to hint I was sleepy. I felt the urge to rub my eyes but blinked instead.

Mama must have known I wasn't ready to go back to bed. She suggested a bubble bath and soft music.

"Of course, I could always lay back down with you, but that won't really help you rest well."

After a pause, she blurted out, "I have it, the perfect thing to help you get back to sleep! Zora, honey, let's take a trip up to the attic."

I frowned, standing without movement, looking at Mama, very confused. I questioned in my mind why she thought I would want to visit the attic in the middle of the night after having a scary dream. Perhaps the lack of sleep was getting to her.

5

# THE Attic

T hurston and I always played in the attic on rainy days. In the daytime, the attic was a great place to be, but at night, with the wind howling through the cracks in the walls and cobwebs in corners peeking out when least expected, it wasn't my idea of a way to help me get back to sleep.

"I don't want to visit the attic."

"Come on, Zora, it will be fine. Trust me. I don't know why I didn't think of this sooner."

I followed her to the door that led up the crickety-cracked, old wooden stairs to the attic. Mama flipped the light switch on and tiptoed step by step up to the attic, with me close behind, the stairs still crickety-cracked.

The attic was full of boxes and antiques that were special to my parents.

For a brief moment, the dark sky with shiny stars beaming down through the sky-light captured my eyes. The stars twinkled so, I froze, mesmerized, until I heard Mama humming an unfamiliar tune.

"Why are we in the attic? Are you going to let me dance until I get tired?"

I loved to dance. I wanted to dance like some of the great women written on my wall: Josephine Baker, Katherine Dunham, and Debbie Allen. Yes, these women's names are on the tree on my wall. As a matter-of-fact, my flesh-tone ballet slippers, pink ribbon decorated CD player, and favorite CD resided in a section of the attic set up as my own personal dance studio.

I hinted to Mama, "I wish I could take dance classes."

"We already talked about this. We just do not have the time right now. Practice with the videos I bought you. Do you know that you come from a lineage of great dancers?"

"What's a lineage?"

"A lineage is just a fancy word for saying family history. It means people in our family from long ago are known to be great dancers."

"No, I didn't know we had great dancers in

 8

our family. I've only known the great dancers on my wall. Are they our family?"

"In one way or the other, yes, they are, and as far as the Travis/Johnson family goes ..." Travis was my mother's last name before she married my father, whose last name was Johnson, "It all started with a girl about your age who lived in Africa, but enough about that;. I need to find something very special to help you sleep."

"What is it?"

"It's a surprise."

My eyes opened wide and my face gleamed with excitement. I loved surprises. I thought about all of Mama's old dolls and stuffed animals that I played with every time I visited the attic with my brother. I hoped the surprise might be the beautiful hand-sewn doll made by her special childhood friend.

Mama wasn't giving me any hints. Maybe it was some jewelry Thurston and I were not supposed to play with but always did. One piece of jewelry I'd always had my eyes on was an emerald stone the size of a shelled walnut dangling inside a golden hoop. Sometimes the light from the sun shined on the emerald so brightly I stared at the jewel as if in a trance.

"Zora, I found it." Mama kept whispering. "Here it is."

Directing my eyes toward the surprise,

my excitement vanished. It wasn't anything to play with or show friends at school. It was old and made me think of sleep. I was too afraid to go to sleep.

"It's just a blanket."

"I know it looks like an ordinary blanket, but it's much more."

Still searching for the significance of the blanket, I asked, "Are these square patches what make the blanket special?"

"No, these patches make this blanket a quilt."

"A what?"

"A quilt. A stitched cover with padding inside."

It was a soft, old, colorfully faded quilt with zigzag shapes. The patterns weren't the typical ones they showed us at school, those made by colonial women, with stars and the American flag on them. No, the patterns on this quilt looked as if they could tell a story. With embroidered pictures, some of specific stones, people, maps, trees like the one on my wall, and one figure that caught my eye, a dancer.

There was a flap in the shape of a hood. "Is this what makes the quilt special?"

"No, the patches and the hood are not what make the quilt special."

   10

"Then what is so special about this ..." I was trying to find a name for the blanket.

"Hooded quilt," my mother answered. "You'll have to wait until you go to sleep."

# CiRCLE DaNCE

We put away all the other items, then the two of us tiptoed down the crickety-cracked stairs back to my room. Mama shook the blanket again and made sure there were no spiders or bugs of any kind before I got into bed. She wrapped the soft old quilt around my body. Maybe the surprise was it smelled good, as if it had come directly from the dryer onto my bed.

"I'm not tired."

"I know, but I have to go to work, and you have school in a few hours. Now, I will stay in here with you until you fall asleep, so put the hood on your head and rest."

Yawning, I put the hood on and lay down

 13

on the pillow. I went to sleep in my bed but woke up peeking from behind bamboo trees. There was a gritty feeling underneath my feet, moving in between my toes. It was red dirt. Maybe it was that color from the warm sun that hid just beneath the sky where the black birds flew above my head.

I could feel my eyes growing wider, focusing on the rest of the scenery. There were straw fixtures that looked like houses. I knew they were called huts. The huts were all lined up in the shape of a circle. In the middle of the circle was a small fire. Around the fire sat three men.

I tilted my head a little to the right as a man beat his hands upon an instrument that reminded me of my father's bongos. Another man played a similar instrument, except it had ivory-colored beads around it that made a whoosh sound. The last man had an instrument I recognized from church. It resembled a tambourine.

With low volume, the three men played their instruments. Slowly, they sped up the pace of the drumming. Children around my age appeared in colors of red, green, orange, and black zigzag and parallel patterns. They danced around the three men.

The pace of the drumming sped up even more. Women wearing flowing blue, black,

green, orange, and gold fabric wrapped around their bodies and heads circled the children. They stamped their feet, clapped their hands, and twirled around. Out came men draped in even more black and colorful cloth. They circled around the women. They leaped high in the air with their hands stretched to the sky.

The patterns in the clothing were similar to a few of the patches in my quilt. All the history embedded in the tree on my wall that Mama insisted I study the past two years came rushing to the front of my memory. I recognized the cloth. It was called Kente.

Every color in the cloth had a meaning. For instance, gold represented royalty, wealth, and spiritual purity. Blue meant peacefulness, harmony, good fortune, and love. Depending on the pattern, it could symbolize knowledge, creativity, and innovation, or conflict, the need for unity, and people coming back together.

I slipped the hood off my head and rubbed the quilt with both hands. Mama told me if I ever had a dream I wanted to get out of or couldn't tell was a dream or real, I should pinch myself.

"Ouch." I massaged my left arm.

She also told me when people were very tired they dreamed of all kinds of crazy things. I must have been beyond very tired.

Nothing changed. The music continued to

play, inviting me to dance, bob my head up and down to the rhythm, sway my shoulders side to side, and pat my feet to the ground. Before I knew it, I stood up and shifted from behind the bamboos and into the crowd.

The dancers had my full attention. I clapped my hands to the beat, lost in the soulfulness of the instruments. I thought about wanting to take dance classes, but remembered what Mama said. Only, I didn't think I could dance like the people in front of me.

Daydreaming myself to the front of the crowd, I heard them say it was time for a dancer from each group to choose someone from the audience to join them. A young girl with dark chocolate skin, the most welcoming smile, bright eyes parallel to the moon, and long braided hair that reached to the back of her knees, grabbed my hand and pulled me out of the crowd and toward the circle.

"I don't know how to dance like that. You should pick someone else," I quickly responded.

The girl took my other hand, put it on my heart, and said, "Dance from here, not your feet."

Puzzled, I squinted my eyes. I moved my eyes left to right then back again.

"Did you tell me to dance from my heart and not my feet?"

"Yes."

16

My mouth fell open. "What language do you speak?"

"It is the African language."

# Native Language

The only African language I knew was from the phrase on my wall in my room: "Dance from your heart, "...*Saw fi wo akoma*." It is spoken by the Asante (Ashanti) people from Ghana in West Africa.

"I don't know African language."

Extending the same soft smile Mama gave me, the girl said, "But you do."

I understood the words she spoke to me.

"We will talk later, but now you must focus within. Forget all that is around you; feel the rhythm of the music. I saw you do it earlier when you were in the crowd."

That was different. I wasn't doing the African dance they were doing. I was simply

moving my body back and forth. Their movement, just like their cloths, meant something,
and I did not know what it was.

"I cannot do it. The steps are too hard."

"We do not say 'I can't' or 'too hard.'
Nothing is too hard, and there is nothing we
cannot do. Please try?"

At a slow pace, the girl taught me the
dance steps the other children had done earlier and told me the story.

"Our dance is a way of life, a way of
thinking, living, speaking. We are a people one
with the earth. The dance you see originated
through movements made by the antelope.
There was a queen mother in our tribe called
Abrewa Tutuwa. During her reign, she sud-
denly fell ill. The gods were consulted and
requested a live antelope be used as a sacri-
fice. The people went to look for the antelope
and were amazed by its jumping and strange
movements. Because the animal was a sign of
the queen mother's health, people wanted to
imitate the movement of the antelope. It is a
dance of celebration."

With little effort, I memorized the movements. It was easy dancing from my heart.
The drummer beat the apentemma, and the
torowa joined in. The crowd clapped their
hands together. It was time for the three

people chosen from the crowd to perform with the dancers.

The girl yelled out to me, "You can do it."

A grin graced my face. I took my cue from the drum and danced. The rhythms and dance, together, created something magical.

I danced hard, but it was as if my feet never touched the ground. Up on one, down on two; as soon as one foot was down the other was up. I leaped in the air like the antelope and then the dance was over.

"Take a bow," signaled the girl. I took a bow. The people cheered me on.

A little out of breath, I asked, "What's your name?"

"Sarai. I'm from the Ashanti village. I want to tell you to come home and eat," she said.

"Huh? I didn't understand. I think you said you want me to come to your house for dinner. Is that right?"

"Yes, right. I'll show you our family. Come quickly."

"But I must get back home soon to let my mother know I'm okay."

I enjoyed African dancing. It was different from the ballet videos I had in the attic. But I didn't know Sarai, and I was always taught to never go anywhere with people I didn't know.

"Who are you here with?" she asked.

"I think I'm by myself, but I don't feel like it because I'm not afraid to be in this place."

"I know. The celebrations are my favorite time of day. Now follow me so you can see the family and eat very good food."

I hesitated for a moment but went with her so I wouldn't be alone. Sarai seemed like a nice girl.

# ASHANTi ViLLaGE

Sarai ran through thick bamboo and sycamore trees, and I followed close behind,
hearing fluctuating rapid and slow tempo
music accompanied by singing I couldn't fully
understand until we were closer to its source.

*Keka mu ma anigye.*
*Anigye! Anigye!! Anigye!!!*
*Kese nyame ma dadaw, ye de ma wo aseda.*

"Shout for joy.
Joy! Joy!! Joy!!!
Great God of old, we give you thanks."

When I emerged from amongst the trees,

 23

I saw a long wooden table with many people gathered around it holding hands. There were so many different types of food.

Many of the women wore adorned braids or cloth as their crowns.

I said to Sarai, "The women here are so beautiful."

The men wore cloths around their bodies, and their hair styles ranged from little black beads to a thick, wool-like texture.

The villagers watched me closely. "I don't think they want me here. They look very serious, mean, and kind of scary."

Sarai assured me, "They are not mad at you. They want to know who you are, so let's join them."

We joined the circle.

"Hello."

With a unified roaring, they replied, "Hello."

I didn't want to be rude. The meal smelled pleasant, and I was hungry. Sneaking a peek at the table again, I noticed dishes resembling the ones at home. There were leaves like collard greens and big reddish-orange potatoes favoring candied yams. There were roasted meats I couldn't quite make out and fruits similar to grapes. My family loved grapes. One time Thurston and I ate so many we got sick. But that hadn't stopped us from eating them since.

A lady with smooth, dark, silky skin; deep black round pupils; long eyelashes; and thick eyebrows asked, "What tribe are you from?"

She was draped in jewels like the type Mama had in the attic. I thought before answering. I knew I couldn't say I didn't know. It was custom for my culture to ask where a person was from. Now I understood why Mama was always telling me to know where I came from and to never forget it, why she put the tree on my wall and made me study it.

Above Mama on the tree there was a man and woman, Grandpa and Grandma Travis. Above my father were Grandpa and Grandma Johnson. Above Grandpa Johnson were my great-grandparents, Mr. and Mrs. Horace Kwame Johnson III, and above them were my great-great-grandparents, Mr. and Mrs. Horace Kwame Johnson Jr. And even though I never met either of them, my great-great-great grandparents were Mr. and Mrs. Kwame Sr., which made my father Mr. Horace Kwame Johnson V. My father didn't care much for the name Horace, so he went by Kwame, like my great-great-great grandfather, and named my brother Thurston Kwame Johnson. I looked at the lady and proudly told her, "I'm from the Kwame tribe."

"Oh wonderful," she said.

She knelt down and kissed me on the hand

and went away. One by one the villagers showered me with kisses. Some of them had tears in their eyes. Others spread their lips into smiles so wide all of their teeth showed.

It was like attending a family gathering with the older aunts and grandparents kissing and hugging me really tight. Sometimes my relatives even grabbed my cheeks, but not so much now that I was almost a sixth grader. They still grabbed Thurston's cheeks, though. He had chubby cheeks. Sometimes I even grabbed and kiss them until he told me to stop and started trying to hit me.

Mama said I provoked him and shouldn't because I didn't like it when family members did it to me. She was right, but I couldn't help it. Thurston was just so darn cute. That's what my grandma always said right before she reached for his cheeks.

Out from the crowd came a man holding a wooden staff. He wore a thick cloth of earth-tone colors. Covering the scar on his forehead was a dark-colored band with bright shades of purple, blue, and red, and part of the fabric was pointed toward the clouds. People bowed to him as he stopped and stood still.

With a deep voice he said, "Zora, beautiful child, come to me."

I stood still, as if stuck in mud, only there was no mud, just the grass beneath me. Sarai

pushed me toward him. He extended his hands to me and knelt just like my great-grandfather, Horace III, who was in his nineties, sick, and in a nursing facility, did.

We visited my great-grandfather every Sunday. When Great-Grandpa wasn't sick, Sunday had been the day we'd go for ice cream. It was one of my favorite things to do. He'd buy me two scoops, even though Mama said I could only have one. Great-Grandpa would always say, "Let the child live a little, Lena. She's a good girl and good girls should be rewarded. Rewarded with two scoops of ice cream."

Mama never argued with Great-Grandpa. She just grinned and let us have our two scoops. Thurston was just a baby then, so he couldn't really have any. Great-Grandpa would hold him in his lap and sneak him a lick here and there.

Now Great-Grandpa couldn't go for ice cream, so we brought it to him. I still got two scoops, but Great-Grandpa only got one, and it was sugar-free. He didn't care much for that kind, but Mama said if he wanted ice cream, that was the kind he had to have.

Thurston always sat close to Great-Grandpa and snuck him a few licks of his regular ice cream. The three of us laughed. Mama probably knew. She just didn't want to spoil our fun.

I ran to the man who looked like Great-Grandpa and hugged him. He picked me up and put me on top of his shoulders like Great-Grandpa used to do.

Everyone shouted blessings my way. After putting me down, the man lifted his staff to the sky. Silence covered the atmosphere. Not even the sounds of animals were heard. He spoke words, then brought the staff down to his right side with a loud thump and said, "Let it be."

A high-pitched shout filled the air. Drums shook the ground. Feet danced. Villagers presented me with gifts. They rendered gold and jewels relative to what we learned in school about Africa possessing a wealth of gold.

One jewel was green. It dangled inside of a golden hoop. I held it tightly in hand. It was from the woman with the jewels like Mama's.

"Oh, thank you very much!"

I was beyond excited to receive such a gift. I would never have to touch Mama's again.

# GREAt PRiNCESS

As the fire grew dim, one by one, the villagers left the celebration, until there was nothing left of the fire but smoldering embers left to be blown into the air by whiffing wind. The villagers departed in different directions. I could not tell where they were going.

Sarai and I were amongst the last group to leave. Right before I was going to ask why we were waiting for everyone to leave, Sarai turned to me, "We must be careful not to draw attention to ourselves. All cannot go where we go."

"Why? Where are we going? Where is everyone else going?"

"You ask many good questions."

 29

Sarai looked around to see if indeed all villagers were gone. She examined me too.

"What is it?" I asked.

"Commoners are not allowed inside the palace unless you are a servant. Everyone else is going to their dwelling place. We are going to the palace."

"The palace? Where queens and kings live? Is there a prince there? I always dreamed I'd marry a prince when I got older."

"Why wouldn't you marry a prince?"

My father called me beautiful princess. He said he was the king, Mama was his queen, and only a prince was worthy of marrying me.

"My mother says I need to wait until after college to even think about marriage. My first priority is getting me an education. I shouldn't expect a prince to rescue me. I don't need rescuing, and I should always know how to take care of myself."

"I am sorry, but you speak of things I do not know. College?"

"Yes, school, scholar."

"Oh, yes. You are to be a scholar. You will be a scholar soon. You do not need to wait years to go to college, right?"

"No, at home we go to elementary, middle, and high school and then college. I'm only in fifth grade. I still have middle and high school

until I get to college. I have seven more years of school."

Sarai looked confused, as if I was the one speaking another language. I was intrigued by the whole palace visit, so I asked, "How far away is the palace?"

"Not far." We had been walking and talking all the while.

"We are almost there."

She pointed to the palace in front of us. We walked another fifty steps to stand at the palace gate. It was dark outside. I could hardly see.

A servant escorted us to a grand room with a bed and a wardrobe. The floor was made of some sort of stone, maybe marble. It was shiny, grey, almost pearl-like. There was a zebra-print rug stretched out under the bed.

The blankets were inviting. I jumped onto the bed, making a blanket angel. I sunk into the nice plush bed until I fell fast asleep.

In the morning, Sarai brought me food. Two tall men stood outside guarding my bed-room door.

"I thought I was dreaming."

"You are home now," answered Sarai.

"What do you mean, home?"

"Last night at the celebration I saw you and noticed your royal robe. Only the princess wears the robe representing all the tribes of

Ashanti. But I did not want to frighten you. I had to make sure you were really her. So I brought you to our family, and they agree you are Zora, the great princess from the Kwame tribe."

I didn't know about a royal robe or being a great princess.

"You mean my hooded quilt?" I asked.

"I am not sure what you call it, but here we call it a royal robe."

I went to grab the quilt to explain to her what Mama explained to me, which, I realized, wasn't much.

"Speaking of royal robe, where is it?"

"It is in the wardrobe."

I went over and grabbed the quilt out of the wardrobe. I put it on and sat on the bed. "I have my own family back at my own house."

"Please do not be frightened. The king and queen will not force you to stay. They only want to see you with their own eyes," Sarai explained.

"Oh, I am not afraid," I fibbed.

I marveled at the palace. It reminded me of pictures from a book Mama bought me, but that wasn't enough to make me want to stay. I decided that immediately following my introduction to the king and queen I'd return home.

The king and queen entered the room. They were both dressed in exquisite clothing

and jewelry commanding respect of all whom their presence graced.

"Hello, Your Majesty," I said, bowing.

"Please, my child, do not bow to us," said the queen.

"Yes," the king agreed, "you do not have to bow to us."

"I'm sorry. I saw it on a TV show at home and thought I was supposed to bow out of respect."

I shook the king's hand and held the queen's hand up to give her a high-five. The guard at the door quickly moved toward me until the king held his hand up in a stop motion. "The child will not hurt us."

The king spoke confidently. People listened to him. The guard returned to his post, then the three of us went on a walk around the palace.

"Why did the big, tall man think I was going to harm you?"

The king knelt down to my level, "Zora, we are the king and queen. We reign over this province. We are royalty. You know what royalty is, right?"

"King, no offence, but I'm ten. I'm intelligent; my teacher says I read way above my grade level. I know and understand big words. Royalty is not that big of a word."

Laughing, he said, "Yes, you are very

intelligent, and why shouldn't you be? You've always had the best."

As we walked around the palace, I tuned the king out. The art on the walls and wooden furniture, some covered in gold, all grabbed my attention, and there were animals I saw only at the zoo roaming free at the palace.

"Is that a zebra?"

"Yes, it is, and there are giraffes and elephants as well," said the queen.

"My backyard isn't big enough to have those kinds of animals. I used to have a dog named Peaches, though."

"Peaches? That's a very interesting name for an animal," said the king. "How did you come up with such a name?"

"I love peaches so I named him that, that's all. What names did you give your animals?"

"We don't give them names, Zora. The animals are not our pets. They live here as in the wild," the queen explained.

"That's cool."

The king and queen glanced at each other. We went on talking as I admired the palace, forgetting about home.

"Ouch." I pinched myself again. I still didn't believe I was in Africa having the greatest adventure ever. How could this be?

"Zora, your eyes look rather glossy. Are you tired?" inquired the queen.

"I guess so, but I thought you wanted to talk to me."

"Yes, we do, but if you are tired, you can take a little nap, and we will talk at lunch, if that's okay with you," said the king.

"I don't really like taking naps. Sometimes Mama says I have to and she doesn't ask or give me a choice. I think naps are for babies and daddies, because my daddy takes naps before he goes to work."

The queen responded, "Well, what about queens? I take naps too; they are very refreshing."

"You take naps? I didn't think kings and queens took naps. I guess a little nap won't hurt."

# At YOUR SERViCE

I was escorted back to my room, and I eagerly situated myself under the hooded quilt. If I could doze into a deep, dreaming sleep, maybe I'd wake up before lunch in my own bedroom at home with my family.

The nap was refreshing, but I didn't recall dreaming. I sat up and stretched my arms and feet toward the sky. There was a gentle knock at the door before it slowly opened.

"Would you like to have your feet washed before lunch, Zora?" It was the queen. That meant I was still at the palace.

"My feet washed? Don't you mean take a bath?"

37

"No, I mean have your feet washed. A servant will wash your feet if you like."

"I never had anyone wash my feet before except Mama."

Maybe the queen meant a pedicure. I wasn't old enough to get one of those. I was supposed to wait until I turned thirteen, then Mama would take me. I didn't answer the queen quickly enough. She clapped her hands two times, instructing the guard to summon a servant to wash my feet. Sarai entered the room with a bucket of water and a rag. Undoubtedly, she was being silly. She inched closer, reaching for my feet.

"Sarai, what are you doing? The queen said she would have a servant wash my feet. You do not have to."

Looking down to the ground, Sarai said, "I am a servant."

"You are a servant? Right. You're so funny. Here, I am a servant too."

I hopped off the bed and knelt on the floor, trying to grab the rag from Sarai. She jumped up and moved away. At the same time, the queen spoke to me in a stern voice, "Zora, get off the floor. You are not a servant."

I stood up. Sarai's eyes moved back toward the marble floor. The queen began to explain, "Her parents were bought by the king and me, but now they are in another place far away. Sarai was left here to serve."

"But last night ... ," I started, speaking before I noticed the fear in Sarai.

Her face begged me to stop talking, so I cleaned up what I was going to say. "Last night you were so kind to bring me here I never would have suspected you were a servant."

The queen continued, interrupting. "Yes, Sarai belongs to me. Sarai, I shall return momentarily. Wash Zora's feet until I return.

"This is not fair. I do not want you to wash my feet."

I succeeded in grabbing the rag from her this time.

"You should tell them you want your parents back or maybe you can go live with your parents. Where are they?" I demanded.

Sarai glanced around. "The ship comes by the sea to where these people put our people on board and take us far away. I want to go far away to see my mother and father, but the queen is very good to me and will be sad if I leave. I don't want to make her sad."

The queen entered the room. "It is time for lunch."

Sarai and I made our way to the eating quarters. There was a table the length of the

room. Servants stood straight as they waited to serve the queen, king, and me.

Patting the chair beside me, I insisted, "Why don't you join us, Sarai?"

"I'm sorry, Zora, but the servants are not allowed to sit at the royal table," the queen said.

"Sarai is not a servant; she is my family."

The king and queen looked at each other. "How do you know this?" asked the king.

"She and I are from the same lineage. I, too, am from the Ashanti Village," I explained.

The king and queen were shocked. They had no idea I knew Sarai was part of my family, but I had figured it out. The night before, the people from the village were my family and her family. What I did not understand was how I could be part of the king and queen's family too.

"You are a very wise, child," remarked the queen. "I have never seen such a child as you. You must have been here before in another lifetime."

"I don't think so, but I have to go home soon. And I would like to take Sarai with me."

Sarai looked at the king and queen in fear.

"It is okay, Your Majesty. I am fine here. Please, Zora, do not trouble them anymore."

"My child, do not be afraid. We knew the day would come when you would have to leave us, and that day is now," said the queen.

Sarai smiled so brightly it seemed the sun shined where we stood.

"Zora, is there anything we can get you for your journey? Surely you will need food and transportation," said the king.

"Thank you."

The queen walked over close to Sarai with an item wrapped in a shimmery pearl fabric. "Sarai, you are free now. I will miss you very much, but I know Zora will take good care of you."

The queen unwrapped the fabric to reveal a beaded doll, which she gave Sarai as a gift.

"Thank you, my queen."

# TiME tO GO

Sarai and I left the palace with food and transportation provided by the king and queen. We traveled ten minutes before either of us spoke a word.

"Oh yeah, oh yeah, uh-huh, uh-huh," I broke out, singing my victory song, feeling good about the success I had achieved, but Sarai did not speak.

"What's the matter?" I asked.

"Nothing."

"Why aren't you happy?"

"I miss my mother and father. I hope to see them again."

"I miss my parents too. I like it here, and

 43

I've met many nice people, but I am ready to go home."

I had a great idea. "Why don't you go to the big boat tonight? You can sneak on, and when it stops, you can get off and find your mother and father."

For the first time since we left the palace, Sarai was happy. We trudged on a little while longer, until our tummies rumbled. We sat beneath a sycamore tree to eat the food prepared for us. We were content.

We must have fallen asleep, for when we woke up, the earth was dark. Maybe someone put sleeping powder in our meal. I didn't recognize our surroundings. We were no longer under the tree. We were on the big boat chained to wood.

All I could do was look up and to the side. Above me was wood and beside me, Sarai. Beside her was another person, a woman from our village. I tried to wiggle lose but couldn't.

"Help! Someone help me!" I yelled. The woman from the village shushed me, but I kept yelling.

"Help! Help me! Stranger danger, stranger danger!" But no one came to my rescue. The only person who addressed my yelling was a man with scruffy-looking hair on his face, dirt under his fingernails, and dirty clothes.

"Shut your mouth before I give you

something to yell about." He stared at me for a moment then left. By then, all the people on the boat were telling me to calm down and be quiet. They spoke in their native language.

A moment later, the dirty man returned with another man. "Speak like you did before, but don't yell," he said.

"Help me, please," I spoke quietly. "I don't belong here. I am—" Before I could finish, the woman from the village told me to shut my mouth and not say anything more, that they could never know I was royalty.

"How do you know I am royalty?"

"Because you are the great princess. You bear a powerful gift. The king and queen sent their soldiers to follow you, and once you fell asleep, they had you captured so you wouldn't take their place in the palace. Now you must travel far away, never to return home."

The men could not understand what she spoke. They thought she was putting a spell on them, so they told her to be quiet too. And she was quiet; the rest of the way she spoke no more. She had said all she needed to say. To me, the men said, "What do you mean you don't belong here?"

I did not know if this was true in Africa, but I said, "I am a child. Children don't belong here."

They ignored my response, "How did you learn to speak English?"

"I'm from America."

"How did you get back to Africa? Are you a runaway slave?"

"No, I've never been a slave."

"I see."

That's all he said, *I see.* Nothing else. That's what Mama said when she was deep in thought. But what had I said to make him meditate so heavily? He scratched his head one last time and left. We only saw him when we needed to be hosed down or fed.

Sometimes my stomach was so sideways I almost puked. I wasn't sure how I managed it, but I did. Then, one day, we arrived in America.

# AMERiCa

We got off the boat for good. Still in chains, we went from one piece of wood to the next. It was like an auction I'd seen on television, where a man spoke very fast, calling out numbers for valuable merchandise, which people bid on by raising their hands. The merchandise always went to the person with the most money. That was exactly what happened every time someone from the boat came off and stood on a thick wooden block. I whispered to Sarai, "Do you see your parents?"

She didn't see them right away. "What if they aren't here? What if I never see them again?"

47

I began thinking about my parents. I wanted to go home. I didn't know how to get home. The quilt brought me there, but I hadn't seen it since we sat under the sycamore tree. I bet the king and queen had the soldiers take it back to the palace.

"Sold to the man over there."

The woman from our village was sold to a man for money. She looked at Sarai and said, "They are not far from here."

The man who bought her pushed her along the way. Sarai lit up with hope. She stood on the block next to me. A woman came along with two girls around our age.

She wore a long, pretty, blue and yellow patterned dress with white ruffles along her neck and sleeves, and white dainty gloves to match. Her hair was clean and curly, and cascading down her back. When she smiled, a tiny dimple appeared in her right cheek. The man shouting out all the numbers said, "Sold to the lady over there."

When we arrived at the house, we were sent to our room. On the bed was my quilt and Sarai's beaded doll. I grabbed my quilt. Sarai grabbed my hand, "Zora, thank you for all your help. I will miss you."

We hugged. "I will miss you."

Sarai picked the beaded doll up from the bed and gave it to me. "I want you to have this."

"I can't. I don't know how these got here, but I think we're supposed to keep them for a while."

"I guess you're right."

Sarai turned the doll over and a little piece of paper hung out of the fabric of its dress. She didn't read well, so I read it for her: "There is clean clothing for you and Zora to wear. Please wash up, put them on, and wait for the servant woman to give you further instruction."

We did as the note said, then we sat on our beds waiting. There was a soft knock on the door. A lady whispered from the other side, "I am here to help you."

Sarai stood straight up. The woman entered the room, closing the door behind her. Sarai rushed over to her. It was her mother. They hugged and sobbed. Sarai's mother cautioned her not to be too noisy. She kissed her head over and over again then held her tight. When they were finished, Sarai introduced me, "Mother, this is Zora."

"Ah, yes, Zora, the great princess of the Kwame tribe. Thank you for bringing my daughter to me. We will go celebrate, then you will return home."

"But I don't know how," I confessed.

"You don't, but I do." She smiled.

"I don't understand. The lady on the boat told me the king and queen had us captured

and shipped here, but they sent the gifts they gave us."

She told me one of the soldiers who captured us was from my tribe. He convinced the king and queen the royal robe and gifts were cursed and whoever kept them would be cursed, so naturally, they insisted the robe and gifts remain with Sarai and me. They promised to pay the men on the boat money to ensure our safe arrival and that our belongings remained safe. Once in America, the men were to look for the woman with fancy white gloves and two young girls. When she received us and our belongings, the men were paid what they were owed.

"No more questions. Follow me," she ordered.

We followed her out the door, through the house to the other small, run-down houses that weren't quite huts like Africa but weren't nice like the house we had just come out of either. A group of people stood waiting for us, then a man walked toward us, toward Sarai. Her father put his hand on both of our shoulders to welcome us. The table was set; we entered the small house and closed the doors behind us. We danced like in Africa. Sarai told her parents of her time without them and our journey to America. It was getting late. Sarai's mother told me to put the hood on my head, think of home, and go to sleep.

# GUESS WHAT?

The sunlight from the window peeked through the curtains, telling me it was morning and time to get up.

I wanted to be home so desperately. With great hesitation, I removed the quilt from the top of my head, just low enough to reveal my eyes. I peered for familiar items. I noticed the tree on my wall, the Barbies, and my posters. I threw the covers back and jumped out of bed. I rushed to my mother's room, but she was not there. My heart raced. I found my mother in the kitchen preparing breakfast. I gave her the biggest hug and she hugged me back.

Still holding her tight, I confessed, "I had a good dream."

51

Mama smiled as she pulled two small green plates from the cabinet and directed me to sit at the table "Tell me all about it," she said.

I began telling her all about the wonderful adventure I had with the quilt. She didn't look surprised.

"What did you learn?"

"I learned a lot!" I exclaimed. "Mama, did you know there are a lot of great dancers in Africa, and that kings and queens live there and they don't give their animals names?"

I went on and on about the boat ride to America and what the ladies told me.

"Mama, in my dream, everyone kept telling me I was a great princess with a powerful gift."

"Well, you are a princess, aren't you?

Of course, to my parents I was a princess; every daughter was a princess, but that wasn't what I meant. I didn't know how to respond to Mama.

She asked me again, this time looking directly at me, "You are a princess, aren't you?"

I didn't know why, but I said, "Yes."

Without hesitation Mama asked, "Did you bring anything back with you?"

"No, but in my dream I received a necklace just like the one you have."

Mama suggested we go back to my room to investigate. Underneath my pillow was the

necklace. I was so happy. My chest heaved and my eyes rose to Mama as I covered and uncovered my mouth in excitement.

"It wasn't a dream! Wait, it wasn't a dream? No, it was definitely a dream. But how could it be a dream?"

Mama held her necklace up as I held mine to assure me it wasn't a dream. Gently pulling me close, speaking with the same excitement, "But let's not tell anyone, Zora. Let's keep it between us for now."

Disappointed but knowing Mama had never steered me wrong before and that there were most likely more lessons to be learned, I agreed. "Yeah, I don't think anyone would believe a story about a hooded quilt that takes you on adventures and lets you bring back gifts."

"Yeah, kind of hard to believe," said Mama.

# THE END

CPSIA information can be obtained
at www.ICGtesting.com
Printed in the USA
LVOW13s0257080917
547997LV00024B/1113/P